ALSO BY JODY LINSCOTT AND CLAUDIA PORGES HOLLAND

ONCE UPON A TO Z

THE WORTHY WONDERS LOST AT SEA

A WHIMSICAL WORD SEARCH ADVENTURE

JODY LINSCOTT

ILLUSTRATED BY

CLAUDIA PORGES HOLLAND

DOUBLEDAY

NEW YORK   LONDON   TORONTO   SYDNEY   AUCKLAND

Special thanks to Mike Linscott for all his help and support.

Our ever warm appreciation goes to our editor,
Jacqueline Onassis, and to Bruce Tracy.

The illustrations in this book are all collages
made with layers of Color-aid paper.

PUBLISHED BY DOUBLEDAY
a division of Bantam Doubleday Dell Publishing Group, Inc.
1540 Broadway, New York, New York 10036

DOUBLEDAY
and the portrayal of an anchor with a dolphin
are trademarks of Doubleday,
a division of Bantam Doubleday Dell Publishing Group, Inc.

DESIGNED BY PETER R. KRUZAN
Library of Congress Cataloging-in-Publication Data
Linscott, Jody.
The Worthy Wonders lost at sea / by Jody Linscott ;
illustrated by Claudia Porges Holland. — 1st ed.
p. cm.
Summary: While following the exploits of the musical group, the
Worthy Wonders, the reader is challenged to find words contained in
other words highlighted in the text.
[1. Musical groups—Fiction. 2. Literary recreations.]
I. Holland, Claudia Porges, 1956—   ill. II. Title.
PZ7.L66315Wo 1993
[E]—dc20 92-43367 CIP AC

ISBN 0-385-47053-3
Text copyright © 1993 by Jody Linscott
Illustrations copyright © 1993 by Claudia Porges Holland

**We dedicate this book
to our kids and our families
—
and to your kids and your families.**

*for Kaeli
& Kylee,
Happy Days,
Claudia Porges Holland ☆*

*to Kaeli -
enjoy !!
Jody Linscott*

This is the story of the further adventures of the Worthy Wonders, a band of talented musicians who travel to distant and exotic lands all around the world. If you have read the first story, *Once Upon A to Z,* you already know who everyone is, but just in case you've forgotten, the members are Andy on keyboards, Daisy playing percussion, and tall Tilly, singer extraordinaire, on vocals. And last (but by no means least) is Daisy's Uncle Ulysses, whose eccentric management methods always lead to strange adventures.

In this story, Uncle Ulysses has bought a salty old wooden sailboat with a motor to take the band to an out-of-the-way island called Dominica-nica-nica, where (if they can find it) they have a big show to perform. It's all very exciting because Dominica-nica-nica is a strange sort of place, hot and tropical, with plants that change color upon touch and 365 rivers, one for each day of the year (except of course for leap year, when they are one river short). People say the orchids on the island are so enormous that you can fit your whole head inside one flower! The Worthy Wonders could hardly wait to see all this for themselves.

They all met as planned, early one Saturday morning, on the dock where their trusty boat was waiting for them. It was well stocked with food, water, spare parts, and other essentials, and they waved goodbye to the assembled crowd of well-wishers and clambered aboard to begin their long voyage south-southeast across the broad ocean.

You can help the Worthy Wonders on their journey by helping them find animals, objects, and all sorts of things along the way. The names of the things are hidden in the colored words—like cat in catch—and they're shown in the pictures too. (There's a key to the words and pictures at the end.)

So off we go . . .

The breakfast foods they ate, you know,
are in the colored words below.

"Let's start this trip off right with a good hearty breakfast," cried Uncle Ulysses. "I'll skipper the boat while you three cook." Andy, Daisy, and Tilly jumped up and headed for the galley but got jammed together in the doorway! Uncle Ulysses screamed with laughter. "What a fruity team," he chuckled as he disappeared up the companionway, waving to several passing boats on the way. When breakfast was ready the three begged him to join them. Then they all raised their glasses and toasted a successful journey.

Under the waves and on the sea bed,

the creatures here are in words colored red.

After breakfast the three joined Uncle Ulysses on deck. Gazing at the water, Andy asked the old codger, "What sort of fish is that out there?" In a crabby voice Uncle Ulysses replied, "That's no fish, it's a bottle. Let's reel it in. Fortunately we can reach it from here." And so they did, pleased at being able to clean up the sea at least a tiny bit. They spent the rest of the day having a whale of a time composing a new song all to do with the natural world, and by early evening the clammy air had made them so sleepy they floundered down to their cabins. During the night they woke to find the boat lurching dangerously. In a moment it strayed into some jagged rocks with a loud crash and began to sink! They heard Uncle Ulysses yelling in a big voice.

The clothes they chose to take, I think,
are sewn right into the words of pink.

"Grab some clothes and abandon ship! We're sinking!" shouted Uncle Ulysses. It was dark and slippery and the three musicians scrambled quickly for their things. Andy emptied his dresser while Tilly searched her closet and took a suitable supply. Madcap Daisy was so shortsighted without her glasses that she ran into the engine room by mistake and wondered how her room got so greasy. Uncle Ulysses invested his precious time by making sure everyone got out safely until he tripped over a hassock and found himself in the water first! The three dove in after him and they all swam for their lives.

The furnishings in this household scene
are built right into the words of green.

Their flight from the sinking boat took them at last to an island that seemed to be in the middle of nowhere. There was absolute bedlam as everyone talked at once, thankful to be safe and sound. "Stop this noise!" shouted Uncle Ulysses. "We need order. I'll be chairman of the meeting. First of all we must have a stable shelter." They all went to work, using whatever they could find, and built an outlandish hut. Insofar as an island home was concerned, it turned out to be fantastic!

"This is okay," shrugged Andy, "but we still have to find Dominica-nica-nica with no boat and no gear."

"Have faith," replied Uncle Ulysses, rubbing the stubble on his face. "Things always have a way of working out." They went to sleep hoping for a miracle.

Some instruments the Worthy Wonders play
appear below in words shaded gray.

Morning came at last. Tilly woke first, sat up, and looked around her. Suddenly she trumpeted right into Andy's eardrum, "Look what the tide brought in!" At the water's edge, ensnared in some sharp thorns, were all their instruments, as good as new! "Hallelujah!" cried Tilly. "Come on, everybody." They rushed to the beach and fiddled around all day building a little stage and getting things organized. When they had finished Andy was so happy he bellowed like a basset hound. "What a voice," laughed Tilly. "It's a good thing he doesn't do any singing."

In the purple words the animals stay,
thinking this is their lucky day.

They practiced on the homemade stage, and the music rang through the island. Curious animals, brave or cowardly, and of all shapes and sizes too, tiptoed doggedly through the dande-lions to catch the strange sounds. "Do you have the feeling we're being watched?" asked Tilly sheepishly, feeling a little rattled.

Daisy, looking about her, suddenly cried out, "Look! We have an audience!" Fixing her ponytail and going to the front of the stage, she shouted to the assembled creatures, "Wel-come to the hippodrome! We are the Worthy Wonders. Please share the show with us."

Flying creatures, old and new,

have landed in the words of blue.

It wasn't long before a crowd of birds, hearing all the commotion, arrived and ducked and dove their way through the palms like acrobats to hear the swanky musicians play. They circled and floated like balloons above the little stage. "Look at that!" cried Daisy, pointing upward.

"What a picture," said Uncle Ulysses, swallowing hard, and added, "My great regret is that the camera went down with the boat."

"My great regret," said Andy, "is that we are supposed to do a show in Dominica-nica-nica today and we don't even know where it is." Tilly acknowledged that he had a point but her voice trailed off as she spotted something out of the corner of her eye.

The names of all the crew, I'm told,
are mentioned in the words of gold.

In the distance was a ship. Tilly jumped up so excitedly that she lost her balance and landed in a patch of roses. Her apron was covered in prickles and her face was as red as a tomato. The others glanced over quizzically. Looking over the stony cliffs, she exclaimed in victory, "It's a ship! Send an SOS!"

Uncle Ulysses quickly remarked, "Normally the lamp would be handy for that, but it's broken, so I have another idea— scream!"

A small boat manned by sailors in blue jackets skated from the ship to the beach. "Ahoy," said the skipper. "We saw a flock of strange birds circling the area. When we came closer, we heard your shouts."

"Saved—and, frankly, just in time," said Andy. "But can you help us get to Dominica-nica-nica?"

"Willingly," the captain replied in a fine Scottish accent. "Follow us." And they set off through the jungle.

A Surprise Ending

"Why are we going this way?" queried Daisy.

"You'll see," answered the skipper mysteriously. After pushing through the trees for some time they suddenly came into the open and found, to their amazement, a stage all set up and ready for them. "Dominica-nica-nica," said the captain with a wave of his hand. "You were here all the time. But hurry—the audience is coming soon!"

Scarcely believing their good fortune, the Worthy Wonders rushed to the stage, took their places, and gave the greatest show of their lives!

THE WORTHY WONDERS

Word and Picture Key

Breakfast Foods

1. tart (start)
2. jam (jammed)
3. cream (screamed)
4. fruit (fruity)
5. tea (team)
6. pear (disappeared)
7. oats (boats)
8. egg (begged)
9. toast (toasted)

Sea Creatures

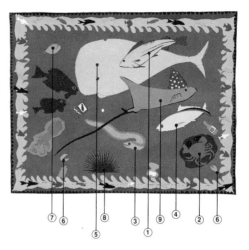

1. cod (codger)
2. crab (crabby)
3. eel (reel)
4. tuna (Fortunately)
5. whale (whale)
6. clam (clammy)
7. flounder (floundered)
8. urchin (lurching)
9. ray (strayed)

Clothes

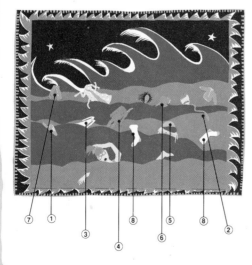

1. slipper (slippery)
2. tie (emptied)
3. dress (dresser)
4. suit (suitable)
5. cap (Madcap)
6. shorts (shortsighted)
7. vest (invested)
8. sock (hassock)

Furnishings

1. light (flight)
2. sink (sinking)
3. bed (bedlam)
4. chair (chairman)
5. table (stable)
6. dish (outlandish)
7. sofa (Insofar)
8. fan (fantastic)
9. rug (shrugged)
10. tub (stubble)

Instruments

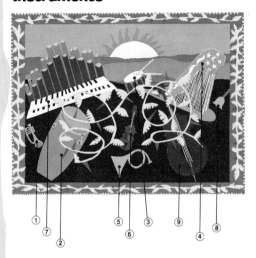

1. trumpet (trumpeted)
2. drum (eardrum)
3. snare (ensnared)
4. harp (sharp)
5. horn (thorns)
6. fiddle (fiddled)
7. organ (organized)
8. bell (bellowed)
9. bass (basset)

Animals

1. stag (stage)
2. cow (cowardly)
3. apes (shapes)
4. dog (doggedly)
5. lion (dandelions)
6. cat (catch)
7. sheep (sheepishly)
8. rat (rattled)
9. pony (ponytail)
10. hippo (hippodrome)
11. hare (share)

Flying Creatures

1. crow (crowd)
2. duck (ducked)
3. dove (dove)
4. bats (acrobats)
5. swan (swanky)
6. loon (balloons)
7. swallow (swallowing)
8. egret (regret, regret)
9. owl (acknowledged)

Names

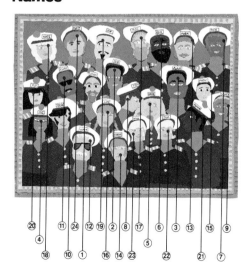

1. Stan (distance)
2. Ted (excitedly)
3. Alan (balance)
4. Pat (patch)
5. Rose (roses)
6. Ron (apron)
7. Rick (prickles)
8. Tom (tomato)
9. Lance (glanced)
10. Tony (stony)
11. Cliff (cliffs)
12. Victor (victory)
13. Mark (remarked)
14. Norm (Normally)
15. Andy (handy)
16. Ann (manned)
17. Jack (jackets)
18. Kate (skated)
19. Kip (skipper)
20. Flo (flock)
21. Frank (frankly)
22. Tim (time)
23. Will (Willingly)
24. Scott (Scottish)